A LITTLE BIT WILD

KNIGHT SECURITY
BOOK 2

SHAW HART

Copyright © 2023 by Shaw Hart

www.shawhart.com

All rights reserved.

No part of this publication may be reproduced, transmitted, downloaded, distributed, stored in or introduced into any information storage or retrieval system, in any form or by any means, whether electronic, photocopying, mechanical or otherwise, without express permission of the publisher, except by a reviewer who may quote brief passages for review purposes. This book is a work of fiction. Names, characters, places, story lines and incidents are the product of the author's imagination or are used fictitiously. Any resemblances to actual persons, living or dead, events, locales or any events or occurrences are purely coincidental.

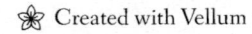

Created with Vellum

WANT A FREE BOOK?

You can grab Sweets Here.
Check out my website, www.shawhart.com for more free books!

She wants to do something wild.

When I first meet Aria Clipton, she's just meant to be a client.

Her mom passed away, and her final wish was for Aria to step outside of her comfort zone more.

She doesn't want to do it alone, so she's hiring me to keep her safe while she does everything on her bucket list.

With each activity that we complete, I fall a little more in love with my curvy redhead.

The wildest thing about this is that I think she might be falling for me too, but my girl is cautious.

When I finally tell her how I feel, will she agree that we're meant to be, or will falling in love with someone she just met be too wild for her?

ONE

Kye

I TURN INTO GATES' apartment parking lot and pull up to his door. We had a late night last night so we're headed into work a little later today. He's not out yet so I idle at the curb, waiting for him. I'm somehow early today but I know that Gates will be down in exactly two minutes. Gates is always punctual. He's also loyal, stoic, and my best friend in the whole world.

I like to say that he's the brother that I never had. We both grew up as only kids on the east coast. I was raised by a single dad who tried his best to make things fun even though we were always struggling. Gates was raised by an alcoholic single mother, and he actually spent more time taking care of her than the other way around. He hasn't been back to see her once, and I can't blame him.

My dad passed away a few years ago. They say heart attack, but I know it was from him just working himself to death. The bank took our house, and I paid to bury him.

There wasn't anything left for me back home so when Gates and I got out, we struggled with figuring out where we wanted to live.

We've been carpooling to work ever since we got to Los Angeles and started working for our old friends at Knight Security. Gates and I were Navy SEALs with Anson and Rhett. They both got out about six months ago and started their own security firm right after. What Gates and I got out, we tried a few different towns before we landed in Los Angeles.

I'm still not really sold on the place, but Gates was so set on it for some reason. When he told me that Dillon might be coming here, I knew that was why he was so insistent that we come here.

Gates has always been in love with Dillon. They were best friends when they were in high school but went their separate ways after graduation. He's always insisted that they were just friends, but anyone can see he's in love with her. I just wish they would both wise up and do something about it.

Gates opens his door and jogs down the steps toward me. He slides into the passenger seat and grunts at me.

"Good morning to you too, sunshine," I say with a grin as I pull away from the curb.

He grunts again, and I just smile as I head down the street toward the Knight Security offices. Gates isn't much of a talker so I'm not surprised by his lack of small talk.

"Anson texted me and said that there's a new client there already," I comment, and Gates nods.

"Makes sense. We wrapped up with the ambassador yesterday," Gates grumbles, and I nod.

"Business is doing well. I wonder if they'll hire more people soon."

"Probably," Gates says, and I roll my eyes.

"It's crazy that you're still single and don't have more friends," I joke, and he just grunts.

Gates and I met in boot camp, and we just clicked. I could talk to anyone, and he wouldn't talk to anyone. We complete each other. When I told Gates that, he made me promise to never say that again.

We went through BUDS training together and then got assigned to the same unit. We've been through five different deployments, three different bases, and countless close calls. It's only made us closer friends.

When Rhett got injured six months ago, I think it scared both of us. Then we found out that Anson was also getting out and decided to join them. We're lucky that they started a company and could hire us, or I don't know what we would be doing right now.

We're all trained on multiple weapons, plus Gates was a medic. So far, we haven't had to fire a single shot. The clients we've been getting have been a pop star, a visiting politician, and an ambassador's family. We just spent the last week driving two tween girls around town to country clubs and fancy restaurants.

I'm grateful for the paycheck, but I'm starting to miss the excitement that came with being a Navy SEAL.

I pull into the parking lot and park in my spot next to Rhett's car.

"Any update on Dillon moving here?" I ask him as I turn the car off.

"Yeah, she'll be here in a few weeks."

"How long is she staying?"

"I don't know."

"*Where* is she staying?"

"I don't know."

"What do you know?" I ask as we climb out of my car.

"That you're annoying."

I laugh as I follow him inside and over to our desks. Anson is on the phone in his office, and I look around for Rhett as Gates gets settled in his office next door to mine.

"Hey, think you can take the new client in the conference room?" He asks me, and I nod as I set my jacket on the back of my chair.

"Sure."

"Thanks; the phone has been going crazy since the ambassador left. I think we have three or four more clients on the books already."

"That's good then," I say as I drop my keys on my desk and glance over at the small conference room.

There's a curvy red-haired woman pacing back and forth in there. Her face is turned away from me so I can't make out any of her features, but she seems agitated, and I wonder what she could need security for.

"What's she in for?" I ask Rhett.

"No clue. She just walked in, and I asked her to wait in the conference room until I had a spare moment."

He knocks on the doorway of my office before he heads back to his, and I take a deep breath as I get ready to greet my very first client.

TWO

Aria

I CAN'T HELP but feel that this is a mistake.

I've never done anything like this. I don't even know where to start.

Does a security company even offer this kind of service?

I shove my hands into the pockets of my jacket and my fingers brush over the papers stuffed there.

My last letter from my mother.

She's why I'm here. It was her dying wish that I do something wild and outside of my comfort zone.

I loved my mother. She was fearless, and I always wished I could be more like her. Unfortunately, I turned out to be the exact opposite of her. I tend to overthink things. I prefer to be alone with my computer than the center of attention. The only things we had in common was our red hair and blue eyes.

Still, I loved my mom, and I would do anything for her, so if she wants me to go do something crazy, then I will.

I'm just going to take back up with me when I do it.

I wish I had a friend I could ask to go with me, but I just moved to Los Angeles from San Francisco and don't know anyone in the area yet. My closest friend here is the Chinese food delivery man. How sad is that?

I sigh, turning and pacing back toward the door. Stepping out of my bubble shouldn't be this hard. I don't even know what I want to do. Something extreme like jumping out of a plane? Cliff diving? Or does just going for a hike count as something wild?

I wish she had been clearer. I wish she had just left me a list. I love to-do lists. I could have easily handled that. I suppose her asking me to think up tasks is also her way of encouraging me to step out of my comfort zone.

She would have laughed when I told her I went to a security company to hire an ex-Navy SEAL to accompany me on my task. She would have loved it. She probably would have encouraged me to flirt with one of the guys here or done so herself.

I laugh at the image, and tears sting my eyes. My throat gets tight and scratchy as I try to hold back my tears.

Do not cry in this conference room! With your luck, now is when they'll finally come in and – SON OF A BITCH!

"Hey there, sorry for the wait," comes a deep voice behind me, and I hurry to wipe the tears from my cheeks.

"Hey," I say quietly, clearing my throat.

I turn around to face the man, and my mouth drops open. He towers over me, easily a foot taller than my five-foot-four frame. His blond hair is a little longer on top but shaved close to his scalp on the sides, and it looks so soft.

"Are you alright?" He asks me quietly, and I meet his bright blue eyes.

He's looking at me with concern, and I clear my throat again.

"I—" To both of our horror, I start to cry.

Run out of here and never look back! My brain screams at me, but before I can take a step, I'm in his arms.

"It's alright, darling. Whatever you're scared of, I'll take care of it. You're going to be fine. I promise," he whispers, and I find myself leaning against him.

I haven't had anyone to lean on or comfort me since I buried my mother a month ago. I didn't even realize I needed it, but being in this hot stranger's muscular arms feels so right.

"I'm not in danger or anything," I mumble when he pulls back. "I'm sorry, this is dumb. I shouldn't be here."

"Why don't you let me be the one to decide that," he says, pulling out one of the chairs at the conference table for me.

I plop down, still trying to dry my eyes, as he takes the chair next to me.

"I'm Kye," he says, holding out his hand.

It's huge, with calluses dotted along the ridge of his palm and on his fingers.

"Aria," I tell him.

I force myself to place my hand in his, and I'm not surprised when goosebumps and shivers race up my arm. He doesn't say anything or react as I let him shake our hands for both of us.

"What's going on, darling?"

"I need a friend."

Why?!? Why is that what my brain tells my mouth to say?

"Oh my god," I groan, sinking down in my chair.

I'm close to sliding off and crawling under the table. I can live here now until I die of embarrassment.

"Easy," Kye says, his blue eyes sparkling as he chuckles and reaches out to tug me back up into the chair fully. "I'll be your friend, darling."

"I shouldn't have said it like that. I'm just not sure that a security company offers what I'm looking for. I don't know who would, though," I ramble, and he nods.

"What are you looking for?" He asks, and it's on the tip of my tongue to say you.

Luckily for me, my brain-to-mouth filter seems to be back on and I keep that to myself.

"My mom just passed away."

"Aria, I'm so sorry," he says, and I can see from the look in his eyes that he means it.

"Thanks. She was... really amazing. She was my best friend and my complete opposite. She wasn't afraid of anything, and I'm afraid of everything," I admit with a smile.

He smiles back at me, and I notice a dimple in his cheek.

Oh, come on, Universe! How is that fair? He already has all the muscles, those freaking beautiful blue eyes, and perfect, straight white teeth, and now you have to add dimples to the mix? He wasn't perfect enough without them.

I stare down at my old jeans and thin t-shirt that says Yale across the front. It's been washed so many times that the e has basically disappeared, leaving Yal behind. Meanwhile, he's in black jeans and a tight green polo that makes his muscles look bigger.

"She wanted me to take a chance, do something wild and out of character. That was her last wish for me," I say, trying to stay focused on why I'm here and not the male model sitting a foot away from me.

"Okay, and you want someone to arrange security for that?" He asks, and I shake my head.

"I don't want to do anything crazy alone."

"Ah, so you want a partner in crime."

"Yes."

"Alright. I can do that," he says easily, and I blink.

"You offer that service?" I ask him, and he grins.

"No, I don't know anyone who would offer that service, but if you want to stay safe while you're doing something you don't feel comfortable with, then I'm your guy. I've spent the last week driving spoiled tweens to their tennis lessons. I was just thinking I could use some excitement, so your timing is perfect."

"Okay..." I say because I'm not sure what to say back to that.

"What did you want to do? Do you have a list?" He asks.

"I wish," I grumble, and he smirks.

"We'll make one."

He drags over a notepad and grabs a pen.

"How crazy do you want to get?" He asks, clicking the pen. "Like skydiving or scuba diving?"

"Does it have to include diving?" I mumble, and he laughs.

"No, we'll do whatever you want," he says easily.

"Um, maybe we... I... you can add skydiving and scuba diving," I say with a sigh, and he laughs.

"What do you want to do?"

"I want to go home, order a burger or some Chinese food, and read a book."

"We can start there. Have you ever had Indian food?" He asks, pushing to his feet, and I blink.

"Uh, no."

"Great. There's a spot right around the corner. Let's go."

He places his hand on the small of my back, steering me out of the conference room and out the front door.

"Be back later!" He calls to his friends, and I can only blink as he marches me outside and down the sidewalk.

"What are we doing?" I ask once we've reached the corner.

"Going to lunch."

"Why?"

"You wanted to get food and eat at home. You step outside of your box and eat at the restaurant. Baby steps."

"I don't know if eating out counts as something wild."

"We'll work on the list while we eat," he promises as he opens the front door for me.

I look around the restaurant as Kye talks to the hostess, and then I'm dragged to a table in the back and handed a menu.

"How spicy do you like your food?" He asks, and I chew on my bottom lip.

"Like not at all."

He nods, and I scan the menu, trying to figure out what half of the words mean.

"What should I get?" I ask him, giving up, and he grins.

"I'll order. You just relax."

I set my menu aside, taking a deep breath, and I'm surprised at how good it feels not to have to make a decision.

I've been doing nothing but that since I graduated and started my own company. I'm an investor, and I run my own firm. I've always been great at investing, researching which stocks or companies to bet on and which to pass. I've stepped back in the last few months, which is one of the reasons why I moved to Los Angeles. I was meant to be taking a break, entering a sort of semi-retirement, and spending more time with my mom.

Instead, she passed just a week and a half into my being here.

Kye orders for us, and I blink, coming back to the present as the waitress heads back to the kitchen. The restaurant is empty except for us, probably because it's only ten in the morning, and I smile. I kind of like being alone with him.

"So, tell me about yourself," he orders, and I grab my napkin, twisting it between my fingers.

"What do you want to know?"

"Where are you from? What brings you to Los Angeles? What do you do for a living?"

"I'm originally from Texas. This tiny town that no one has ever heard of. I own my own investment firm, but I've been stepping back a bit, and I came to Los Angeles to be closer to my mom."

His eyes soften when I say that, and I swallow, looking away from him.

"I lost my dad a few years ago. It gets easier," he says quietly, and I glance back at him.

"It doesn't feel that way," I admit, and he nods.

"I know, but I promise that it will."

He nods, holding my gaze, and I try to smile.

"I hope so."

The waitress comes back, dropping off our water, and I grab my glass.

"Any ideas on what you want to add to the list?" He asks, changing the subject.

"I just want to do something wild and exciting," I finally say, and he grins, leaning his elbows on the table.

"And you trust me to pick the activities?" He asks, and I blink.

"Yes," I admit, and I think I surprise us both with that answer.

I barely know this guy, but I do trust him. He seems like a good man, someone who is charming, caring, and completely trustworthy.

"Good. We'll get started right now then," he says as the waitress comes back over with our food.

As I stare down at all of the plates of curries littering the table, I can't help but wonder what I've gotten myself into.

THREE

Kye

"ARE you sure you don't want backup?" Anson asks as I get ready to leave the Knight Security office the next day.

"I'm sure. I know you have paperwork to finish, and I thought that Rhett said another new client was coming in today," I say as I head for the door.

"Yeah, alright, let us know if you need anything."

"Will do!" I call back as I head out to my car.

It's a beautiful day here, and I smile as I hop in my car and head toward the airfield. I've been smiling since I left Aria yesterday. There was just something about her that stuck with me.

When I noticed that she was crying when we first met, I didn't even think. I just reacted, wrapping my arms around the curvy redhead and pulling her against me. From there, my protective feelings for her only grew.

I always thought that when I met the one, I would just

know, and that's what I felt yesterday when I met Aria. She's meant to be mine. I know it deep in my gut.

I haven't told the other guys about what she hired me for. I just said she wanted a bodyguard for a few days and that I could handle it. I know that Gates suspects something. He's been eyeing me more lately, and when I told him that I couldn't drive him to work today, he raised an eyebrow at me. In Gates' language, that means that he's on to me.

I wanted to tell him yesterday about her. It feels weird not to share everything with my best friend, but this all is still so new. I don't want to tell him that I met the one if this is all going to stay strictly professional. I mean, Aria is grieving right now. The last thing that she needs is me hitting on her. I just have to hope that she can feel this between us too.

I pull up outside the West Coast Extreme office and park, looking around to spot Aria. I had wanted to pick her up, afraid she would chicken out on me, but she had insisted on driving. I had made her promise that she would be there, and we even shook on it before she left yesterday.

There's no sign of her yet, but I'm early. I park next to a newer-looking Audi and climb out. I just happen to glance over, and I laugh when I see Aria slouched down in the driver's seat. She looks miserable, and I reach for the passenger door handle and climb in beside her.

"It won't be that bad," I promise.

She jumps at me breaking into her car but relaxes when she sees that it's me.

"But how do you know that?" She asks, eyeing the plane taking off like it's a snake.

"I've jumped out of planes like a hundred times. A

buddy of mine owns this place. He's an ex-Army ranger. He knows his shit. We'll be safe."

She nods, but she looks pale.

"Or we can start with bungee jumping," I say, nodding over to the bridge that's set up on the property to do just that.

West Coast Extreme is like an adrenaline junkie's playground. There's bungee jumping, base jumping, skydiving, and zip lining, all spread out over a hundred acres along the coast. The main building where we check in is pretty small, just big enough to store the supplies and a small office.

"You think this is fun," Aria accuses me, and I laugh.

"It *is* fun," I insist, and she shines the tiny flashlight attached to her keys in my eyes.

"Uh-huh, and how long would you say you've been experiencing these delusions?" She asks with a straight face.

"Come on. You're going to have a blast."

I climb out of her car, and she sighs but follows me as I walk up to the front door.

"I'm not going up in your plane!" A pretty blonde shouts as soon as we step inside. "Are you crazy!"

"See, this girl gets it," Aria whispers to me, and I try not to laugh as I look over to my friend, Huck.

He's behind the counter, giving the blonde an amused smile.

"You want me to take you for a different kind of ride?" He asks, and I laugh into my hand, trying to pretend that it's a cough.

"Ugh, in your dreams!" She spits at him, and she glares at me as she storms out.

"Making all the ladies swoon still, I see," I tease Huck as we head for the counter.

"Not all. Just one," he says, staring after her.

I'm dying to ask what the story is there, but I have a feeling that if we don't get up soon, Aria will bolt just as fast as Huck's blonde friend did.

"Ready to go skydiving?" He asks us, and Aria just stares at him with a blank face.

"We sure are!" I enthuse. "Aria here could barely sleep last night; she was so excited."

"It wasn't excitement. It was terror," she grumbles, and I laugh as I start to fill out the paperwork that Huck slides my way.

"I just need you two to fill out these forms. I'll be taking you up myself. You'll be tandem jumping with Kye," Huck tells Aria, and she nods, gripping the pen tight as she starts to write down her information on the form.

I pass the clipboard back to him, and he nods towards a side room.

"Gear is in there. I checked it myself, but I know that you'll want to double-check it," he says, and I clap him on the shoulder before I head over to where the parachutes are waiting.

"It's okay. You're in good hands with Kye," Huck tells Aria, and I can't help but peek back at them as he tries to reassure her. "He's done this stuff a million times."

She nods, seeming a little less like she's walking to her death, and I smile as I double-check the bags and gather up the harnesses and glasses.

"All set?" Huck asks, and I nod.

I take Aria's hand in mine as we walk out the back door and over to the waiting plane.

"I'll let Kye here tell you what to expect while I do my check," he says, and I nod as he walks over to the little Cessna plane.

"You'll have to put this on," I say, holding open the harness for her to step into.

I pull it up her legs, trying not to get turned on as I go, and then tighten it around her waist. I pull my own harness on, and she glances around.

"It's pretty. I guess I won't mind dying here," she says, and I laugh.

"We're going to be fine. I'm going to hook you up to me once we're in the plane. You'll have to wear the glasses on the way down."

She nods, taking them from me as we head toward the plane.

"There's going to be a bench in the plane. We'll sit on that with our legs on either side. Once we're in the air, I'll hook up our harnesses, and then when we hit the right altitude, I'll open the door, and we'll sit on the edge like this," I tell her, hopping up into the plane. "Then I'll count to three, and we just fall out."

"Uh-huh," she says, looking a little queasy.

"All set?" Huck calls as he climbs into the plane.

"Yep."

I jump down, boosting Aria into the plane before she can protest. She sits, looking down at me slightly, and I smile, gripping her hips.

"If you change your mind, it's fine. We don't have to do any of this."

I know she's been joking around a lot and obviously scared, but I can see the determination in her eyes too. She wants this.

"Okay," she says, and I smile.

She crawls into the plane, and I jump up, sliding the door closed and joining her on the long wooden bench.

The plane engine roars to life, and she jumps.

"Take slow, deep breaths," I advise her, and she nods.

We can't talk much more than that. It's hard to be heard over the plane, but she reaches back, gripping my hand as we start to taxi.

"I've got you," I yell as I scoot closer to her on the bench, attaching our harnesses.

She nods, gripping my hand tighter, and I squeeze hers back.

It takes almost no time at all for us to take off and reach our jump height. I wrap my arms around her waist and look over her shoulder at her.

"Still want to do this?" I yell, and she takes a deep breath.

"I trust you!" She yells back, nodding.

I don't think she gets just what those words do to me. Every time she says them, my heart leaps in my chest.

I nod and reach over, opening the plane door.

"See you on the ground!" Huck yells back to us, giving me a thumbs up as we move to sit in the open plane door.

"Ready?" I yell, and she nods. "One... two..."

I push us out before we can get to three, and I hear Aria suck in a deep breath as we start to fall. I put my arms out, loving the feel of the wind whipping by. The free fall doesn't last very long, and I want to soak up every minute of it.

Soon enough, it's time for me to pull the parachute cord. The fabric unfolds above us, and we jerk to a stop, starting to slowly glide down to the ground.

It's dead quiet now, no noise reaching us this far up, and I take a deep breath.

"How are you doing?" I ask Aria, and she laughs.

"I'm good," she says, sounding surprised.

I grin, letting her soak in the view.

"Want to steer?" I ask her, and she laughs.

"Are you crazy?"

"Too wild?" I ask, and she seems to think about it.

"Alright, what do I have to do?"

"Reach up and grab these handles. If you pull this one, we go this way," I say, demonstrating. "And if you pull this one..."

"We go that way. Got it."

Her hands grab the handles over mine, and I leave mine there as we slowly lower back to the ground.

"We want to aim to land over there," I say, pointing with my toe to the open field next to the office building.

"Okay," she says, and I help her pull on the left handle to steer us that way.

"When we land, you want to lift your legs to a ninety-degree angle so they're parallel with the ground. I'll handle the rest."

She nods, and I steady us as the ground approaches.

"Lift now," I say, and our legs rise.

I put my feet down, walking slightly forward as the parachute hits the ground behind us. I make sure that Aria is stable before I unhook our harnesses and spin her around in my arms.

"How was that?" I ask, and instead of answering, she launches herself at me, wrapping her arms and legs around my body.

"Thank you," she whispers against my neck, and I nod, holding her tightly.

"I've got you," I promise, and she nods.

"It wasn't so bad. I guess," she admits, and I grin.

"Good to hear. I'll ask Huck if he wants to add that quote to his website."

She laughs, and I let her slide down my body to the ground.

"What now?" She asks, looking around.

"I'm going to roll the parachute back into the backpack, and then we'll go find Huck. Did you still want to do the bungee jumping today or come back a different day?"

The skies are starting to darken, but if we hurry, we might be able to do the bungee jumping before it starts to rain.

"Can we come back?" She asks, and I nod.

"Of course. I'll try to get it scheduled with Huck before we leave."

She nods, sitting in the grass as I gather up the parachute.

"You've really done that a million times?" She asks, and I laugh.

"Well, maybe not a million, but we did it a lot in training and then on some missions. Some friends and I would just go do it for fun too."

"It was... cooler than I expected."

"That's what I love to hear," I tease her, and she throws a leaf at me.

"Did you always want to be in the military?" She asks me after a moment, and I shrug.

"I wanted to get out of my small town. There weren't many jobs there, so if I didn't want to work at the local factory, I would have to leave. I didn't know what I wanted to do, though, and I didn't have the money or the smarts to go to college."

"I don't believe that," she says softly, and I shrug.

"I never liked school all that much."

I saw the Yale sweatshirt yesterday. My girl is a genius, but as I admit that I wasn't the best at school, I see no judgment on her face. It makes me relax more as I start the process of folding the parachute back into the bag.

"School was all that I was good at. I'm terrible at making small talk. I never saw the point in drinking or going to parties. It may surprise you, but I've never had that many friends."

"Well, now you do," I say, and she smiles.

"Can I help with anything?" She asks, but I shake my head, waving her off.

"I've got it."

We enjoy the cool breeze as I finish up. The sky is quickly darkening, and the sun dips behind some clouds.

"Why don't you head inside? I have a feeling that it's going to start pouring any min—"

Just like that, the skies open up and it starts to pour. Aria laughs, and I reach down, pulling her to her feet. She holds my hand, and we run back to the West Coast Extreme office building together.

"Just in time," Huck says as we run inside.

"I know. That storm came out of nowhere."

He nods, and I drop the parachute back in the supply room before I head up front.

"We'll have to reschedule the bungee jumping," I tell him, and he nods.

"Come back anytime. I'll talk to you later," he tells me, and I wave before I grab Aria's hand, and we race out to the parking lot.

She stops suddenly, and I look back, wondering if she got hurt somehow, but she's smiling.

"Is dancing in the rain crazy?" She asks me, and I grin.

"Sure," I say, pulling her into my arms.

We sway together, occasionally spinning or dipping her

back, and she laughs as we slowly make our way over to our cars.

If I had any doubts, that moment solidified it. This strangely cautious girl who is coming out of her shell with me; she's the one for me.

Now I just need to make her realize that too.

FOUR

Aria

I'M NORMALLY SO good at thinking things through, but I guess when Kye is involved, my brain takes some time off. That's the only explanation I can think of for why I would agree to wear a freaking wetsuit in front of this Greek god.

The dang thing took me almost twenty minutes to get on, and then when I saw my reflection, I wanted to scream. I tried to convince myself that I only looked like a dying beached whale because I was so sweaty from wrestling this thing on. I don't know why I thought I would look better once I was wet. Oh, and trying my hardest to balance on a surfboard.

"That's it! You almost had that one," Kye says.

He looks like he's modeling for a surfing magazine as he sits on his surfboard, and I try not to ogle him as I paddle back toward him.

"You're a terrible liar," I wheeze, and he laughs.

"I'm serious. You almost stood up on that wave."

"Uh-huh," I pant. "You go ahead and take the next one."

"Are you sure?" He asks, looking like an excited puppy dog.

"Oh yeah."

I try to nod, but I have a feeling that I look more like a deranged bobblehead.

How is even my neck sore and tired?

Kye paddles toward the next wave, and I try to catch my breath. We've been out in the water since six am, and it has to be close to ten now. He had spent half an hour showing me how to pop up on my board, and then we had gone out to try it.

It has not been going well for me.

I've managed to stand up on my board twice, and both times I immediately fell off. The other dozen times, I either managed to kneel or somehow fall off my board without even getting that far.

Still, it's kind of been fun. Kye is so happy to be out here, and he's been so supportive. He even told me he likes my wetsuit, though he was probably just being polite.

I cheer as Kye stands up, and I find myself beaming as I watch him. He's surprisingly good at surfing for only having done it a few times. He told me he had learned when he was on a training assignment in Hawaii a few years ago but hasn't had a chance to do much of it. That kind of made me hate him, but he's so dang nice that it's hard to stay mad at him.

"Show off," I call when he heads back my way, and he laughs.

"Want to try one more? Then we have to get ready for our scuba diving excursion."

I groan, and he grins.

"When are you feeding me?" I ask him.

"We'll hit up the taco truck on the way to the docks."

He points over to the food truck pulling into the lot, and my stomach growls. I'm too hungry to be embarrassed, and get ready to start paddling back to shore.

"You can do this one!" Kye says, and I take a deep breath, waiting for the wave.

I pop up, and to my and the passing seagull's surprise, I actually manage to stay up. I'm wobbly as hell, but I laugh as the wave crests behind me.

"I did it!" I yell, spinning around to look at Kye, and that's when I lose my balance and crash into the waist-high water.

I'm too pumped on adrenaline and excitement to care, though, and I pop back up, thrusting my arms into the air. Kye is cheering, and I can see him grinning at me from here.

I walk up onto the shore as he catches his own wave and rides in. He hops off his board, sprinting through the water toward me, and then I'm in his arms.

"That was awesome! You're a natural!" He cheers, and I laugh as he spins me around. "Whoops!"

He sets me down, and we have to untangle our ankle straps. He takes mine off and then his own, and then he pulls me in for another hug.

"That was really good. I'm impressed."

"Thanks," I say, feeling the blush spreading across my cheeks and down my neck.

"Alright, tacos, and then we need to return the boards to the stand and get on the road."

I nod, grabbing my own board and following him across the sand. There's a line starting to form at the food truck, and I let Kye take my board as I peruse the menu.

"I'll go drop these off. Be right back."

I nod, watching him jog across the sand and over to the

little rental shack. He makes small talk with the attendant, and they both laugh.

Envy unfurls inside of me. *What would it be like to be able to talk to anyone?* Kye is so confident and charming. He can make anyone feel at ease. *I wish that I could be more like that.*

"Know what you want yet?" He asks me as he jogs back over to my side.

"Yeah," I say, nodding distractedly.

I want to be his.

It's been two and a half days with Kye, and I feel like he's already made me a better person. I've tried so many new things. I've laughed more than I can ever remember doing. I wake up each day with a smile on my face, excited to see what he has in store for me, excited just to see him.

Someone like him would never go for someone like me, though. We're complete opposites. Besides, he could get any girl that he wanted. Why would he choose to be with someone like me?

"Can I get the breakfast burrito with extra bacon?" I order, and Kye moans.

"That sounds so good. Make it two."

My jaw drops at hearing him make that sound, and I'm pretty sure that I drift off into fantasies of him making that noise when we're doing something else because the next thing I know, he's nudging me out of the way and paying.

"Hey! I wanted to pay for breakfast," I object.

"You can get the next one," he says easily, and I sigh.

"I'd stuff money into your pocket right now if you had any pockets."

"Noted," he says with a laugh.

Our food is up soon, and then Kye is leading me over to his car and opening my door.

"We can just stay in the wetsuits. The dock isn't far, and we'd just have to put them back on."

I nod, sliding into the passenger seat and unwrapping my burrito.

"Oh my god! This is so good," I groan.

"I know, right? Anson told me about this place, and I come by for a burrito at least once a week now."

"We need to come back every day," I say, taking another big bite.

"Deal."

He starts the car and drives us to the dock while I finish my burrito.

"You've been scuba diving before?" He asks, and I shrug.

"Twice. My mom took me when I graduated from college and then again last year. I'm definitely not an expert or anything."

"But you know the basics."

"Yeah."

He nods, pulling into a parking spot and climbing out. I'm not as nervous about this activity, and I'm not sure if it's because I've done it before or if I just feel more confident with Kye by my side.

I walk ahead of Kye up to the front door and turn around to tell him that this is actually where my mom and I went the last time we went scuba diving. When I look back, I'm surprised to see Kye staring at my ass. He licks his lips, his bright blue eyes darkening, and for a second, I could swear that it almost looked like he wanted me.

He looks up at our eyes meet. My cheeks start to heat again, but he just smiles and winks at me.

"You've got killer curves, darling," he says, and pleasure blooms in my chest.

He likes my curves? My body?

No one has ever told me that before. I don't think anyone has ever given me a second look, and here Kye is telling me that he likes my curvy frame like it's no big deal.

"Thanks?" I say, and it sounds more like a question.

"You sound surprised," he comments.

"I am," I admit.

"Why? You have to know that you're freaking gorgeous. A hottie with a body," he says with a smile.

"Please never say that again," I groan, and he laughs.

"Now you sound like Gates."

"Who is Gates?"

"My best friend. He works at Knight Security too. I keep forgetting that you didn't really meet the guys," he says as he opens the door for me.

I nod, waiting while Kye walks up to the front counter.

This place reminds me of my mom. We were only here once, but she loved it. She talked about getting an aquarium so she could see the fish we saw every day for like a solid month. I can almost hear my mom's voice in my head as I look around.

She would tell me to flirt with Kye, to take a chance and see where things lead, but I can't do that.

Can I?

FIVE

Kye

ARIA IS SMILING, and she seems lighter as we head back up the dock toward the parking lot. She actually seemed excited about scuba diving, and I'm glad she seemed to enjoy herself so much.

It was cool to see her have so much fun. When she had told me that her mom had taken her here before she passed, I had been worried that she wouldn't want to stay, but it seemed to make her feel more connected to her.

"Are we finally getting out of these wetsuits?" She asks with a sigh, and I try not to imagine her stripping for me as I nod.

"Yeah, we can change over there, and then I'll drive you back to the office."

"Sounds good."

She grabs her bag out of the trunk of my car, and I lead her over to the changing stalls. I know she still has her swimsuit on under her wetsuit, and I try not to picture her wiggling her way out of the tight latex as I strip off my suit.

I pull on my jeans and a t-shirt and head out to wait for Aria. When she still isn't out five minutes later, I approach the door.

"Are you okay? Need me to give you a hand with anything?" I call, praying that she doesn't hear the lust in my voice on that last question.

I clear my throat as she lets out a long breath.

"It took me twenty minutes to get into this thing. It's going to take me an hour to get it off," she grunts, and I smile. "Just go on without me. I live here now."

"So dramatic," I tease, and she growls.

"I bet yours just peeled off like it wasn't even the tightest thing that you've ever worn in your life," she accuses, and I try to bite back my grin.

"Something like that. Come on; I'll help you out."

The door unlocks, and she swings it open, glaring at me slightly. Her face is flushed, and her red hair has come out of the bun slightly.

"How, man? How did you get it off so quickly?"

"I've had a lot of practice in these. Here, turn around."

I rest my hands on her shoulders, turning her around. She meets my eyes in the mirror, reaching to move her hair to the side as I reach for the zipper.

Unzipping her wetsuit feels so intimate, and I clear my throat, trying to think of something to clear the tension and distract me, but my mind comes up blank.

I pull the latex to the side, swallowing a groan when I see the strings of her bikini.

Just work fast. Drive her back to the office and say goodbye. Then you can go home and jerk off to this.

I peel her arm out of the wetsuit and then move on to her other one.

"I think I've got it from here," she says quietly once the wetsuit is bunched up around her waist.

"Are you sure?" I ask, and Jesus, is that my voice?

It's suddenly turned deep, husky, and filled with so many wicked promises.

"Yeah, thanks," she says.

I take a step back, and she turns to face me. She's looking up at me, her ripe lips right there, and I can swear she wants me to kiss her. It's written all over her pretty face.

What is the protocol for dating a client? How pissed are Rhett and Anson going to be?

I weigh the pros and cons in the blink of an eye before I realize that I would risk anything to have Aria.

I take another step back toward her, and she licks her lips, that pink tongue swiping along the plump bottom lip as she tempts me more.

"Aria," I whisper, my hands coming up to cup her face.

"Everything alright in there?" Comes a voice as they knock on the door.

Aria and I both jump, leaping apart as much as we can in the small confines of the changing stall.

"We're fine!" I call back, and I look back to Aria.

She's watching me, and I swallow.

"I'll let you get changed," I say, and she nods.

I step out, wondering if I just messed everything up between us. Did I just miss my chance with her?

I have to believe that that's not true.

It takes Aria another five minutes to get changed, and then we walk silently back to my car. I get her door for her, and she gives me a small smile as she slips inside.

"Fuck," I murmur as I close her door and round the hood.

I need to fix this.

"Bungee jumping tomorrow?" I ask as I start the car, and she nods.

"Sure. I think the weather is supposed to be nice."

I nod, and we drive back toward the office in silence. I just can't seem to think of anything to say. I don't want to push her into anything. I know she's grieving, and maybe she just got wrapped up today, which is why she almost kissed me.

I need to talk to Gates, Rhett, and Anson. They'll be able to help me figure things out. Plus, it will finally get Gates off my back. He's been watching me like a hawk for the last few days, trying to figure out what's going on.

We pull into the Knight Security parking lot, and I park close to her car.

"Hey," I say, stopping her before she can bolt from the car. "Do you want to do something crazy tonight?"

Her eyes almost bug out of her head, and I immediately start to backtrack.

"Food! Do you want to get something to eat with me tonight!" I rush to tell her, and she sags back against the seat.

Her face has gone almost as red as her hair, and now I want to know what she thought I was suggesting... and what her answer would have been.

"Um, sure," she finally agrees, and now it's my turn to sag back against my seat in relief.

"Cool. I'll pick you up around six?"

"Okay. I'll text you my address."

I nod, and we both climb out of my car. I wait until she's driving out of the lot before I turn and head inside.

I don't get very far.

"So that's what's going on with you," Gates says, scaring the crap out of me.

"Jesus! Are you stalking me?"

"I just got back from lunch," he says easily, and I roll my eyes.

"Did you get me anything?" I ask hopefully, and he tosses me a sandwich. "You're the best."

He grunts in response, and I unwrap the sandwich, taking a big bite.

"So," he says, and it's not a question. It's a nudge.

"So, she's the one."

"Good for you," he says, and I can tell he's happy for me.

"Now it's just you left. Why don't you call Dillon?" I ask him, and he turns on his heel, stalking inside.

I follow behind him, and we almost run right into Rhett and Anson.

"Hey, how is the new client?" Rhett asks me.

"She's good."

"What have you been doing?" Anson asks.

"We went surfing and then scuba diving," I say, and everyone's head snaps to look at me.

"No fair," Rhett whines, and Anson laughs.

"What's going on?" He asks me, and I take another bite of my sandwich.

"She hired me to go with her on this quest. We're doing extreme things together because it was her mom's last wish for her," I explain.

Rhett and Anson seem a little confused about the security aspect of this. I don't blame them.

"And she's paying us for that?" Anson asks.

"Um, well, we never actually talked about that," I admit.

"He's in love with her," Gates says when Rhett opens his mouth.

"Oh," Rhett says like that explains everything.

"Okay, cool, man. Can't wait to meet her," Anson says, clapping me on the back as he heads outside.

"Yeah, bring her by for dinner soon. We're headed out to meet a client. See you tomorrow," Rhett says as he heads out after Anson.

"Thanks for that," I tell Gates, and he grunts again.

"You were going to over explain everything. My way was simpler."

I smile, following him over to our offices. He closes his door in my face, and I laugh.

"Calling Dillon now?" I ask him through the glass, and he flips me off.

His phone rings, and I see him glance at the screen. I can tell by his expression that it is Dillon, and he looks up at me, glaring.

"Shut up," he grumbles, and I laugh as I head to my office next door.

I finish my sandwich as I try to figure out where to take Aria on our date tonight. By the time I leave for the day, I'm feeling confident that tonight will go my way.

Please, let it go my way...

SIX

Aria

"YOU LOOK BEAUTIFUL," Kye tells me as he smiles at me across the table.

He's told me how pretty I look tonight at least three times since he picked me up, and each time, my stomach flips and my whole body starts to feel too warm.

I like his compliments and his attention.

"Thanks. I've never been here before," I say, looking around the restaurant.

We're at a little Italian restaurant a few blocks from the coast. It's charming with its ivy-covered walls and flickering candles on each table.

"I found it a few weeks ago. Gates and I came here and then realized that it was more of a date spot than a casual friend dinner," he says, and I smile, but inside I'm wondering at his words.

Is this a date? I dressed up like it was, though I've never actually been on a date before. Still, I dressed up more than

I normally would. Kye has been acting like it is too. Between his nice dress shirt and him picking me up.

Do I ask him?

"The ravioli," the waiter says, interrupting my internal freakout as he sets our dishes in front of us. "Is there anything else that I can get for you?"

"No, we're good," Kye says.

I'm practically drooling as I stare at the plate of ravioli in front of me. Kye ordered some penne dish that looks delicious too. We both dig in, and I moan as the flavors of tomato, basil, and garlic hit my tastebuds.

"So good," I say, and he nods, popping a piece of pasta into his mouth.

We eat in silence for a moment, both of us enjoying our food.

"Is Italian your favorite food, then?" I ask him.

"I don't know that I have a favorite. I just like food," he jokes, and I grin.

"Same. What did you usually eat on deployments?"

"It depended on where we were. They have a cafeteria on the bases, and sometimes that food wasn't that bad. If we were stationed somewhere that wasn't a war zone for a few days, then we would try to head off base to try out the food."

"Did that happen often?" I ask him.

"No. Usually, just when you were en route to another base. We'd go to UAE or Germany and be there for a day or two before we left again."

"It's cool that you've seen so many places."

"Do you like traveling?"

"Maybe? I haven't been to that many places outside of the United States. Even then, when I was traveling, it was always for work.

"And that's not really a vacation since you only see conference rooms," he finishes for me, and I nod.

"Exactly. I remember being so envious of all these people flying all over the world for meetings. I thought it must be so cool to go to New York or London. Then I became that person and realized that by the time you land, you're tired and hungry. You might see a few restaurants, but you're in meetings all day, and by the time you get out, it's usually late. I never got to do any touristy stuff."

"Not even as the boss?" He asks me.

"No, not really. My mom would force me to slow down; to go on little day trips with her. That was about all of my downtime, though."

"How are you liking retirement then?" He asks carefully.

"It's been..." I trail off.

How has it been?

Sad and lonely, at least in the beginning. Since I've met Kye, though, things have been looking up.

Can I tell him that, though? Will it freak him out?

"It's been better. I'm not so stressed anyway. Well, when I'm not being shoved out of an airplane and all that," I tease, trying to lighten the mood.

"I didn't shove you," he says with a laugh, and I grin.

"That's how I've been describing it to people."

"Oh, good," he says sarcastically, and I giggle.

I finish off my ravioli and lean back in my chair, stuffed.

"Ready for dessert?" Kye asks, and I groan.

"Not even a little."

"I'll get it to go."

"I think I love you."

The words just pop out, and we both freeze once I've

said them. We're staring at each other, me in shock and him... well, it looks like he's trying to gauge if I meant that.

My eyes dart to the door, wondering if I could outrun him. I'm sure he'd catch me and even if I managed to get away, he drove us here.

"I'd catch you," he says, and I look back at him.

"I wasn't thinking about running," I lie.

"Liar. It was written all over your face," he says with a grin, and I start to relax.

"That wasn't my 'I'm going to run away now' face. It was my 'I wonder if they have good tiramisu here' face," I tell him, and he rolls his eyes, but he's smiling.

The waiter comes back, and Kye orders one of each dessert to go.

If I wasn't in love with the guy before now, I definitely am now.

Kye pays the bill as the waiter boxes up our desserts, and he looks up at me. Our eyes lock, and he stares at me for a beat.

"What's that look mean?" He asks quietly, and I swallow hard.

I'm sure that my feelings for him are written all over my face, and I blink, trying to clear the lovestruck look from my eyes.

"Just thinking about that tiramisu," I lie, and he nods.

The waiter comes back and drops off our boxed-up desserts, and Kye stands, offering me his hand. For some reason, it feels huge to slip my hand into his. He's been grabbing my hand and hugging me since we met. Why would it be so different now?

Deep down, I know the answer is because this feels more intimate. This whole dinner felt like a date.

I hope that it is.

We head out to his car, and he opens the passenger door for me.

"Thanks," I murmur, and he nods as I slip inside.

The drive back to my house is over far too quickly, and as he pulls up in front of my house, I realize I don't want our night to be over. For the first time in my life, I want someone. I just don't know how to navigate this.

Do I invite him in? Kiss him? Throw myself at him and beg him to make me come so many times that we both lose track?

So probably not that last one...

If we do sleep together, then what is this? Are we dating? Is it just a fling? A one-night stand?

What could be wilder than a one-night stand?

I chew on my bottom lip as Kye turns to face me.

"I'll walk you to your door," he says, and for the first time since I've met him, Kye sounds reserved.

Is he thinking about being with me too?

That thought seems like almost too much to wish for, but as we start to head up the front porch steps of my house, it feels like it could be a possibility.

"Do you want to come in?" I ask him hoarsely as we stand in front of my front door.

"Sure," he says, and I could almost swear that his grip tightens on the take-out bag of desserts.

I unlock the front door, letting us in, and as soon as the door closes behind us, I'm on him. The take-out bag falls to the ground as I press my body against his and kiss him. I have to stand on my tiptoes to reach, but it's worth it to have his mouth on mine.

"Fuck," Kye groans, gripping my waist and tugging me up further.

When he realizes I can't stretch anymore, he spins us, lifting me in his arms so our mouths are level.

"That's better," he says as my back lands against the front door, and I nod, eager to have his lips on mine again.

"Kiss me," I beg, and he happily obliges.

I cling to him, my legs wrapping around his lean waist as his lips claim mine. He tastes like basil and tomatoes, and Italian food suddenly becomes my new favorite.

Kye's fingers dig into my ass, and I wonder if I'll have bruises tomorrow. For some reason, I hope so. I want to wear his brand; I want to look down and see the reminder of this night for days to come.

"Bedroom," Kye asks against my mouth, and I hum in the back of my throat.

I need to answer him, but I don't want to pull away for even one second. Who would have thought that the quiet, studious girl that all of my classmates and colleagues know would be such a little minx?

"Hall," I mutter against his lips, and he grunts, lifting me and starting to carry me through the house.

I bought this place because it was close to the water, and I knew my mom would love it. She always dreamed of owning a place on the beach, and I made that dream come true. I wish that she had been able to enjoy it more, but being here now still makes me feel close to her.

We make it into the master bedroom at the end of the hall, and I sigh as Kye lays me down on the bed.

"Aria," he starts, and I know he's going to ask me if I'm sure, but I don't want him to. I don't want to think tonight. I don't want to weigh all of the pros and cons. I just want to enjoy myself for once.

"Fuck me. Please," I tell him, and his blue eyes darken with want.

"Yep," he says, and then he's reaching for my clothes.

I sit up, helping tug my shirt over my head. He reaches for my bra, and I go for the button of his jeans. We're a jumble of clumsy hands, but we manage to make it work.

"Jesus," Kye moans when my breasts are free from the lace bra, and I've never felt more beautiful than in this moment.

He's not looking at the rolls of my stomach or my wide hips. He's just looking at me, at all of me, and it's clear that he likes what he sees.

"Kye," I say, and he nods, pulling himself out of his daze.

"I've got you," he promises.

He pulls his shirt off, and I shimmy out of my jeans. Then I'm before him in just my panties. He's staring down at me, his jeans unbuttoned but still around his hips.

"You're the most beautiful thing that I've ever seen in my life," he says, and I can see the honesty and need swirling in his eyes.

"You're hot as fuck," I tell him, and he laughs.

Then he's on me. He kisses me as his hands find my breasts, and he cups the soft mounds in his hands.

"So damn soft," he whispers as he starts to trail kisses down my neck.

I close my eyes, letting Kye take charge. His licks a path across my collarbone, and I shiver. When his mouth wraps around one sensitive nipple, my brain shuts off, and I just feel.

I want to stay in this bubble forever, where it's just Kye and me. I love feeling the weight of him on top of me. I love each of the callouses on his fingers as he runs his hands over me.

"More," I beg, and he smiles against my skin as he starts to kiss lower.

He kneels on the side of the bed, gripping my hips and dragging me closer to the edge. Then he's pulling my panties down my legs and tossing them aside.

"Have you ever had a man here before, darling?" He asks.

He seems strangely on edge, and I wonder if he'll leave if I admit he's my first. Still, I can't lie to him.

"No," I whisper, and he sags in relief.

"Thank fuck," he groans.

I want to ask him what that means, but before I can, he buries his face between my legs, and my brain empties of all thoughts except what he's doing to me.

"Oh, oh, oh!" I chant when his lips wrap around my clit.

My back bows off the bed, and I come hard. I should probably be embarrassed at how fast it happened, but all I can think about is getting him to do that again.

"Your turn," I say when he kisses his way back up my body.

"I need you too damn much," he says, pushing his pants and boxers down his legs and kicking them aside. "Lay back, darling, and let me love you."

I scoot back into the center of the bed as Kye prowls up the mattress after me. He's so big and strong, looming over me. It makes me feel small and safe, something a plus-size girl like me rarely gets to feel.

"I'll go slow," he promises as his cock nudges against my opening, and I nod, spreading my legs wider for him.

He kisses me as his dick sinks an inch or so inside me, and I relax in his embrace.

"So fucking tight, darling. It's so good," Kye groans, and I wiggle under him, wanting to take more of him.

He pushes forward, giving me another inch, and he tenses as he brushes against my virginity. His eyes lock with mine, and I nod, wrapping my arms around his neck.

I want this. I want him.

He thrusts forward, and I suck in a sharp breath at the sudden feeling of being so full. There's a pinch of pain, but it's there and gone in the blink of an eye.

Kye is kissing me, promising it will only hurt this first time and telling me how perfect I am. I tighten my hold on him and wrap my legs around his waist.

"Oh!" I gasp as he sinks even deeper inside of me.

"Jesus," he chokes out into my neck, and I smile.

"Are you going to show me a wild time?" I ask him, and he chokes on a laugh but gives me what I want.

His pace is slow at first as he lets me get used to his size and rhythm. Soon though, we both start to lose control, and as it slips, his thrusts become harder and more frenzied as we both chase our release.

"Kye! I shout, my fingers tangling in his hair as my orgasm slams into me.

"Fuck, darling... Aria," he moans, and I watch as he finds his own pleasure.

He's even more handsome when he's coming. His tan skin now has a light flush, and his blond hair is tangled and twisted from my fingers.

He's gorgeous.

His movements slow, and he blinks his eyes open, his blue ones locking with mine, and my heart kicks against my ribcage as a new emotion swells inside me.

I know it then.

I'm in real trouble here.

SEVEN

Kye

NEITHER OF US has mentioned last night.

I'd like to think that it's because things are just so natural between us that we don't feel the need to bring up the mind-blowing sex that we had just twelve hours ago. Something in my gut is telling me that that's not why we're not discussing it, though.

I don't know how to bring it up, either. Do I try to make it a joke and keep it light? I could just say something like, 'hey, I'd loved to have sex with you again,' but that might be weird.

What if she doesn't want to? What if she thinks that last night was a mistake? I'm not sure that I could handle that.

"I'd just like to point out that I'm like barely even out of breath," Aria pants as we hike up the trail.

"I know; I'm so proud of you. I'll have to sign us up for a 5k next."

"Whoa, let's not get crazy now," she says, and I laugh as I follow her up the trail.

She's so funny. I think I've laughed more with her than anyone else in my entire life.

Dad would have loved her.

I smile at the thought, wishing they could have met.

"We're almost to the top," I tell her, and she nods, picking up the pace a bit.

We're on one of the more deserted trails. It winds its way along the cliffs next to the coast. It's supposed to be one of the easier trails, and I'm glad to see that Aria isn't having any trouble with it.

We pass by a guy and his dog coming down and wave. He's the first person that we've seen since we started hiking almost an hour ago. I kind of like that we have this time to ourselves. I hate sharing her with anyone, and it's nice to feel like we're the only two people on Earth for a bit.

"Whoa," Aria whispers, and I move to stand by her side as we look out over the water.

"It makes you feel small, doesn't it," I comment, and she nods.

"My mom always loved the water. She said that's why she moved here and put up with the Los Angeles traffic."

"It's worth it," I say softly, and she nods.

We stand side by side, staring out over the calm water. It seems to stretch on forever, and I let it calm me. I've always loved the water and swimming. It's one of the reasons why I became a SEAL instead of going into a different branch of the military. I think lately, I've forgotten to enjoy it, though. Going surfing and scuba diving with Aria the other day was the first time I had been in the water in months.

"Do we have to go back down now?" Aria asks, and I shake my head.

"We can take a break up here for a little bit. Come on; there's a spot over there."

I take her hand, leading her over to the small clearing. The grass is soft, slowly blowing in the wind as we take a seat with our backs against the giant boulder there.

"This would be a good picnic spot," I comment.

"Yeah, I'm surprised that there's not more people out here."

"I don't think that many know about this trail. There are so many around here."

She nods, and I pull out the water bottles and trail mix in my backpack. She starts to pick out the candy from the trail mix, and I just smile as I twist open the top of my water.

She's got a light sheen of sweat coating her skin, and I can't help but think back to how she looked last night. I debate bringing it up again now. Maybe we should talk about it, but I don't want to make her feel uncomfortable. Especially when we're miles away from the car.

"You look pretty," I tell her, and she looks at me like I'm crazy.

"I'm covered in sweat and probably more than a few bug bites," she tells me, and I just smile.

"Beautiful," I sigh, and she rolls her eyes, but I can see she likes the compliments.

"Crazy," she mutters, and I scoot closer to her.

"You want to do something crazy?" I ask her.

"I'm not jumping off this cliff," she tells me, and I burst out laughing.

"Not that crazy," I clarify, and she eyes me with curiosity.

"You got something else in that bag?" She asks, and I shake my head.

"I was thinking something more along the lines of you letting me eat that sweet pussy right here."

"Here?" She whispers, looking around like she thinks a group of hikers will suddenly pass by.

"Yeah. There's no one else out here. We're tucked away, so even if someone did come up, they wouldn't see us. Plus, it could be a little reward for making it up here."

"Little," she snorts, and I laugh.

"My dick loves the compliment," I tell her, and she blushes.

I start to move back. I'm so sure that she's going to tell me no and that we'll go back to eating and joking around, but she surprises me.

"Alright, but I'm not the only one getting naked. I get to do you, too," she says, determination bright in her eyes.

"Deal."

Easiest decision that I've ever made.

She's giggling as we start to strip, and I can't help but feel lighter and happier than I have in ages.

I always feel this way around her, I realize.

"You first," she says, dropping to her knees, and I push some of her red hair back behind her shoulders.

"So eager," I try to joke, but my voice comes out sounding rusty with need.

"I want to try it," she says, and I push my boxers down, freeing my cock.

It's hard and pointing straight at her, and I'm prepared to talk Aria through it, but she reaches out, wrapping her hand around my length and giving me a pump.

"I can't believe that this thing fit inside me," she marvels, and pride swells in me and my dick.

She licks the tip, and my knees almost buckle. Seeing

that reaction seems to spur her on because she licks her lips, opening her lips wide and taking me into my mouth.

"Oh, fuck," I groan, and she smiles around my dick.

Her head starts to bob as she tries to take more of me, but I'm too big for her. She can only get about half of my cock into her mouth, but that's fine with me. Seeing Aria on her knees, her lips stretched wide around my dick, is heaven. It's my ultimate fantasy.

"Just like that," I praise her as she wraps her hand around the remaining inches and moves it in time with her mouth. "Fuck, that's good."

She moans, and the sound sends vibrations racing up and down my spine. I'm close to coming already, and I need to make this last.

"I need you. You're going to lay back in that grass and let me get one orgasm in my mouth, and then I'm going to fuck you," I tell her, and she nods.

Her eyes are filled with need, and she hurries to lie back on the soft grass. I'm on her in a second, my head buried between her legs, and I lick her sweet pussy. She moans, her cries echoing around the forest, and it's like a symphony to my ears.

She's got a hair trigger, and just like last night, she comes in under a minute. I know that we'll need to work on that, to make her hold off so that her orgasm is stronger, but for right now, it works in my favor.

She's still coming when I thrust inside her, and she screams my name as I pound into her.

"So. Damn. Perfect," I grunt out with each thrust, and she nods, her fingers scrambling to find something to hold onto in the grass.

"Kye, oh! Please," She begs, and I know we're both close.

"Come with me," I command her, and she cries out as her orgasm rushes through her.

Watching her come, feeling her pussy clamp down around me, triggers my own orgasm, and I come deep inside her.

I roll over onto my side, careful not to crush her as we both lay in the grass, trying to catch our breaths.

"Wow," she whispers, and I grin.

"Uh-huh," I pant out, and she pushes my shoulder.

We rest side by side in the grass, both catching our breaths and enjoying the post-orgasm glow. Soon the wind starts to pick up, and we hurry to get dressed before someone stumbles upon us.

"We should get back home," I tell her, and she nods, her face still flushed.

The trip back down seems to go faster, and Aria and I stop to check out the local wildlife on the way. Things between us seem easy and light.

That changes, though.

I can't put my finger on where, but sometime on the drive back to her house, things between us start to shift. That fun energy starts to fade and an awkward tension is left in its place.

By the time I pull up to her house, Aria seems different, more closed off or distant, and I can't figure out why.

Was it something that I did? Something that I said?

"I'll see you tomorrow?" I ask as she hops out.

"Uh-huh," she says distractedly, and I frown as I watch her head inside without a backward glance.

I want to chase her inside and demand that she tells me what's going on, but I doubt that would go over well. I take one last look at the house before I pull out of the driveway and head home.

Maybe she wasn't feeling well, or she forgot about a meeting or something. I'm sure that everything will be better tomorrow, I reassure myself.

I sigh as I pull onto the highway.

Aria is right. I am a terrible liar.

EIGHT

Aria

"UGH," I groan as soon as the door is closed behind me. "I blew that."

I slide down the wood, sitting on my butt as I stare around my empty house. It was such an amazing day. I woke up in bed with the man of my dreams, and then we grabbed those delicious breakfast burritos on the way to his apartment. Even the hike he dragged me on wasn't bad, and it had been worth it for the view and the incredible round of sex.

Then somewhere on the hike down, it all went downhill.

I couldn't turn my brain off. I started to freak out, wondering what the heck is going to happen between us when this is all over.

I have feelings for Kye. I'm in love with him, but does he like me back, or is this just a fling for him? He doesn't strike me as someone who would sleep with all his clients, but what do I know? I lost my virginity to him less than twenty-four hours ago.

I push myself off the ground, hoping a hot shower will help clear my head. I peel myself out of my clothes and toss them in the hamper, ignoring the rumpled sheets on my bed as I head into the bathroom.

I crank the water on, letting it warm up as I stare at my reflection in the mirror. I've never been great at social situations, but surely, I can figure out what to do here.

I step into the shower, trying to work through the problem. The water feels amazing on my sore muscles, but it doesn't help to untangle the mess in my head.

By the time I get out of the shower, I'm even more frustrated, and I can't stand to be in my big empty house. It feels stale and boring without Kye's laughter bouncing off the walls.

I grab my keys, heading for the door.

I'll go grocery shopping. Then I can come home and comfort eat.

I know I need to talk to him, to lay it all out there so that I know where I stand, but that seems too scary. Being with Kye is the happiest I've been in a long time. I don't want to lose him.

I sigh as I grab a shopping cart and head down the first aisle. I grab some chips and pretzels and then make my way down the next aisle. I'm debating between Oreos and Milano cookies when someone says my name.

"Aria, right?" A guy asks, and I blink.

"Um, yeah, sorry, do we know each other?"

The guy has black hair and dark blue eyes. He towers over me, and I look between him and the pretty blonde-haired girl at his side. They're both smiling at me, looking like they know me, and I can't place either of them.

"Yeah, sorry. I'm Rhett, and this is Quinn. I own Knight Security with my friend, Anson. You were in the other day," he explains, and I try to place him.

I remember someone greeting me, but I was so wrapped up in the letter from my mom and then in Kye that I don't remember what they looked like.

"Oh, right, sorry," I say, and he smiles.

"No worries. We only met for a second. Kye has been talking about you a lot," he says, and my stomach drops.

Is that a good thing?

"All good things," Rhett rushes to add, and I wonder how panicked I just looked.

"Oh, good," I say weakly.

"Are you coming tonight, then?" He asks, looking at my cart, and I frown.

"Coming where?"

"Oh, sorry, I thought Kye would have invited you. We told him too, but you know how he can get," he says.

"We're having a dinner with our friends," Quinn tells me. "You should come. Here, give me your number, and I'll text you the address."

I rattle off my number and my phone buzzes a second later.

"It's not until six. Hopefully we'll see you there!" She says, and I like her right away.

"Sure. Should I bring anything?"

"Just yourself," Rhett says.

"Alright."

I wave at them and watch them until they head down the next aisle.

Great, now I have even more questions.
Why didn't Kye invite me? Did he really just forget?

Should I show up tonight? We left things kind of weird, so maybe surprising him isn't the best idea.

I kind of want to meet his friends, though...

I grab the Oreos and Milano cookies, deciding that I will need all of the comfort food I can get if I want to make it through tonight.

I only hope Kye is as happy to see me as his friends just were.

NINE

Kye

I WAS SO PREOCCUPIED this morning that I completely forgot to invite Aria to our dinner tonight. By the time I thought about it, it was too late. She would never be able to make it across town in time now.

I wish she could be here, but maybe it's better if she isn't. This way, I can talk to my friends about her, and maybe they can help me figure out what to do in this situation. Should I just see where things go and pray that she doesn't get tired of our little trips? Or should I just tell her how I feel and hope that I'm not moving too fast for her?

I've been debating the two options in my head all day. I want to just tell her that I love her, but I'm worried that I'll scare her off and lose her forever. For once in my life, I'm being cautious, and it's driving me crazy.

I park in front of Anson and Lottie's house and climb out of my car. It looks like everyone else might already be here, judging by their packed driveway. There's a party happening two doors down, and the entire street seems to be lined with cars. I grab the pies from the passenger seat and head up the front walkway.

"Oh, thank god you guys are here," I say when I walk inside.

"In our house?" Anson asks drily, and I grin as I kick off my shoes next to the door.

"I really need to talk to you guys about Aria," I say, looking up and locking eyes with her. "Aria! Hey."

She's standing in the living room, looking at me with an amused smile, but I can see the worry and anxiety starting to swirl in her blue eyes.

"We invited her if that's what you wanted to talk about," Rhett says, and I nod.

"Good, I was going to say I completely forgot to ask her to come tonight," I lie.

Lottie bustles over to my side, grabbing the pies from my hand.

"Fix this," she hisses at me, and I nod.

"Yep. Plan to try."

"Oh god," she mumbles, and with that glowing endorsement, I paste a smile on my face and head over to where my girl is standing.

"Hey," I say, stopping in front of her.

"Hey," she says, gripping her glass tighter.

"Need a refill?" I ask, and she nods.

"Sure."

We walk silently into the kitchen, and I see Lottie shove Gates out when we head that way. He grumbles, but when she nods not so subtly in our direction, he starts moving.

"Hey," Theo says as we join him in the kitchen.

Theo is Anson and Rhett's friend from when they were

kids. He's some hotshot lawyer here in Los Angeles, and occasionally, Rhett and Anson can threaten or bribe him to come to these things. The guy is a total workaholic, but he seems like a solid dude.

"Hey," I say, nodding my chin at him.

"Oh my gosh, Theo! Get out! Read the room, man!" Lottie yells at him, and he rolls his eyes, stomping out into the living room.

"Should we talk outside? Or did you want to stay here and just let them eavesdrop?" I ask Aria.

"Please stay here!" Rhett calls, and I laugh as Aria points over her shoulder to the back door.

"Outside works," she says.

She's trying to be cool and easygoing, but I can see her nerves starting to show. She's worried about what I have to say, and I wonder why. What could she be nervous about?

"Sorry for just showing up here," she says as soon as the back door closes behind us.

"No, I'm glad that you're here. I really did just forget to invite you this morning," I tell her, and she seems to relax slightly.

"So, what's up?"

"Are you alright?" I ask her quietly, and her eyes shoot to mine.

She can't seem to stand still. Her fingers keep flexing and twisting in the sleeves of her shirt.

She looks away, swallowing hard, and worry starts to grow inside me.

"Aria, what's going on?" I ask; all thoughts of telling her that I want her more than I want, my next breath leaving my head as I take a step closer to her and pull her into my arms.

"Tell me what's wrong, and I'll fix it," I promise, and she tenses in my hold.

"I..." she starts, and I hold my breath as I wait for her to finish that sentence.

TEN

Aria

"I... I LIKE YOU," I blurt out. "A lot."

Great. I couldn't just leave it at I like you? Just had to add that a lot in. Why do I hate myself?

I close my eyes, wincing. Man, I wish that I was better at this. I wish that I could be smooth and charming like Kye. He probably thinks that I'm a total dork.

Why would he be interested in someone like me? Oh my gosh, did I just ruin everything?

I find the courage to peek at Kye, and my mouth almost drops open when I see him grinning at me.

"If you start laughing right now, I will die of embarrassment," I inform him. "I mean, telling a guy that I like him is way out of my comfort zone," I ramble on, and that only has him grinning wider at me.

"Your mom would be so proud of you then," he says softly, and my heart melts at his words.

He's right. She would be proud of me for admitting that

I liked Kye. She would be proud of me for doing so many things that terrified me this whole week. I always wished I was brave like her, and I got that wish this week.

I know that she would love Kye and approve of us being together. She would have been pushing me to him all week if she was still here. Tears start to sting the back of my eyes, and I blink, clearing my throat as I try to stop them from falling.

"Thanks," I whisper, and his grin softens.

"And for the record, I love you too," he says, and this time my mouth does drop open.

My heart seems to stop beating in my chest, and the only thought in my head is that I would like to get off this rollercoaster now.

How did we go from me being terrified to tell him that I liked him to Kye telling me that he loves me?

"Whoa, hold up. I didn't say that I love you. I said that I liked you."

"A lot," he interjects.

"Like," I stress, and he just smiles at me knowingly.

Oh, he's lost it.

Is this how dating usually goes? Oh my gosh, we weren't even dating! I was paying him to hang out with me. Except, I never actually paid him for this last week...

Have we been dating this whole time? I've never been out with anyone before, but I always assumed I would recognize when I was on a date. I thought the guy who asked me out would say the actual word, which would be a big indicator, but Kye never did that.

Do people really fall in love so fast? Is this crazy?

YES! My brain screams at me, but it feels so right. I've been following my head my whole life. Maybe it's about time that I started following my heart.

The heart that currently feels like it's going to burst out of my chest.

I stare at the crazy man standing in front of me. The one who convinced me to step outside of my box and start living life. The one who made me feel beautiful and cared for every second we were together.

I've known that I liked Kye since I met him. He's so unlike anyone else that I've ever known. He's smart, thoughtful, hot as hell, and funny. He always seems to be in a good mood, and I love that. He can make me laugh more than anyone else.

He's the first person I think about when I wake up and the last before I fall asleep. I don't want to spend a moment without him and --

"Holy shit. I love you," I blurt out, and he laughs.

"Uh-huh, I know. And I love you too."

"This is crazy. This is so far beyond wild," I tell him, and he just laughs again.

"Maybe, but that doesn't make it any less real."

"I know," I admit, and he reaches out, pulling me into his arms.

We stare at each other, and I can see that an idea is forming in that crazy head of his.

"Want to do something even wilder?" He asks, and I find myself grinning back at him.

"What did you have in mind?"

ELEVEN

Kye

"THIS IS CRAZY," Aria says as I tug on her hand.

I'm worried that she's changed her mind, but when I look back, she's grinning.

"You don't want to do something wild with me?" I ask, and she just smiles wider.

"Let's go."

We laugh as we jog into the courthouse and join our friends. We went down to city hall and filed for our marriage license a few days ago, and now it's time to actually tie the knot. I had thought that maybe Aria would want a big wedding or a more formal ceremony, but she insisted that she didn't. She told me that she didn't want to be the center of attention in front of a room full of people we barely knew, so it's just our friends and us at the courthouse.

"Oh, I love your dress!" Lottie says as we join them in the hall outside the room where they do wedding ceremonies.

"Thanks. It was my mom's," Aria tells her.

"It's gorgeous," Quinn tells her, reaching out to squeeze her hand.

Aria and I are both dressed up. She has a knee-length white lace dress on with a little blue purse. When I asked, she said that it was her something blue. I'm wearing the only black suit that I own. Aria had tried to convince me to wear my dress whites, insisting that I looked so handsome in my military uniform, but I wanted her to be the only one in white today.

I look around, seeing that all of our friends, even Gates, dressed up too. It means a lot to me that they're here and they made the effort.

"Ready to go in?" Anson asks and I nod.

"I wish your mom and my dad could have been here for this," I whisper to Aria as we follow the others inside.

"Me too. But they're with us in spirit."

She squeezes my hand, and I lean down, stealing a kiss as we head up to the counter to check-in.

We pay the fee, and then we're filed into an even smaller room where the Justice of the Peace waits for us.

"Shall we get started?" He asks, and I make sure all of our friends are inside before I nod to him to start.

"Dearly beloved, we are gathered here today," he starts, and I tune him out.

I've never seen anything more beautiful than Aria right now. She's staring up at me with love and excitement swirling in her pretty blue eyes. She looks alive and hopeful, and I can't help but fall even more in love with her.

I hate that her mom passed away, but I'm so grateful that her passing led Aria to me. I know that we're getting married fast and haven't known each other for very long, but when you know, you know. I've known that Aria was the one for me since we met. There was just something about her that called to me.

"Do you," the officiant says, and I blink, focusing back on the ceremony. "Take Aria Clipton to be your lawfully wedded wife?"

"Yes, I do," I say, almost before he can finish asking.

I slip the ring onto her finger, marveling at how perfect the diamond looks. I smile as the officiant turns to Aria.

"And do you take Kye—"

"I do," she blurts out, and I grin, squeezing her hands in mine.

She slides the ring onto my finger, and I flex my fingers, getting used to the feeling of it there.

"Then, by the power invested in me, I now pronounce you husband and wife. You may kiss the bride."

Our friends cheer as I dip Aria back and press my lips against hers. She wraps her arms around my neck, and I can feel her grinning against my mouth as we stand back up. We turn to face Rhett, Anson, Gates, Lottie, and Quinn, and I raise Aria's hand into the air.

"Woohoo!" Quinn cheers.

"Congratulations," Gates says, smiling happily at us.

"Thanks."

"Should we get something to eat?" Lottie asks, rubbing her very pregnant belly.

"Yes, please!" Aria says, and I laugh.

"Italian?" I ask her, and she bites her lip.

"How about burritos down by the beach?" She asks, and I can't help but tug her back into my arms.

"God, I love you," I say as I kiss her again.

"Ugh!" Our friends groan, and I laugh as I intertwine our fingers as we head out.

"Love you, wife," I tell her, and she beams up at me.

"Love you too, husband."

I squeeze her hand in mine as we head out into the sunshine.

TWELVE

Aria

FIVE YEARS LATER...

"SHE'S SO PRECIOUS," Dillon coos down at my daughter, and I smile.

Already the pain and stress from labor are starting to fade from memory.

"I'm just so excited that she's finally here. I was starting to get impatient," I admit, and Kye leans over and kisses my forehead.

We just welcomed our daughter, Louise Elton McArthur, into the world a few hours ago, and I'm already so in love with her. Kye seems to be just as infatuated. He's barely let any of our friends hold her.

He's been freaking out since he found out that we were having a girl. I had finally talked to him, and he admitted that he was worried about being a good dad to a little girl.

He was so used to being around guys that he feared she wouldn't think he was any fun. I had tried not to laugh at that. Everyone loves Kye, and I'm sure our daughter won't be any different.

I already know that Kye is going to be an amazing father. He's been taking care of everything for the last nine months. I'm pretty sure our entire house was childproofed within an hour of us finding out I was pregnant. He had called Gates, Rhett, and Anson, and they all came over to help. The girls and I had just laughed and watched them.

Luckily for me, my pregnancy was pretty easy. The only thing I struggled with was coming up with a name and wishing my mom was here to meet her grandbaby. I have the sweetest husband, though, and when I talked to him about it, he just smiled and suggested that we name her after my mom.

I cried for about an hour after he said that. I don't know how I got so lucky. It still blows my mind that Kye is head over heels in love with me.

He's been the most amazing husband. He's helped me take a step back from the company, and now I'm just the CEO in name, mostly. I have people who run the day-to-day things so that I can relax and spend time with my family and friends.

He makes sure that I still step outside of my comfort zone, though he's been trying to cram me back in that safe box that I used to live in for the last nine months. I swear, he would bubble-wrap me if he thought I would let him.

We're fully settled into our little house on the beach. We've even been going surfing more, although lately, it's been more just wading into the water. Being so close to the ocean somehow makes me feel closer to my mom too.

When I told Kye about my mom loving the water and

wanting an aquarium, he surprised me by building one in the house. I know that she would have loved it, and I love him for thinking of it.

My mom would have loved Kye. He treats me like a queen and is so thoughtful and sweet. They would have got along great, and I wish she was still alive to meet him. I know that she's smiling down at us, though, and that helps.

"We should let you get some rest," Gates says, and I smile.

I didn't want to say anything, but my eyelids have been getting heavier and heavier. I was in labor for almost twenty hours, and now that the adrenaline is wearing off, I'm ready to get some sleep.

We've all grown so much closer in the last five years. For the first time in my life, I have friends. Lots of them, even. We hang out, have dinners, or girls' nights. It's been incredible, and I love that my family has expanded.

Knight Security is going strong, and Kye still loves working there. They gave him the next two months off so he can be home with me, and I'm looking forward to it being just the three of us for a little bit.

"We'll be back first thing tomorrow," Dillon says, and I nod.

"Let us know if you need anything!" Lottie offers.

"We will," Kye says as he walks them out.

He's back a second later, little Louise sleeping soundly in his arms, and I smile sleepily.

"You're not going to put her in the bassinet, are you?" I ask.

"She's comfortable here. I just want a little more time with her. The books said it helps with bonding," he says, and I grin.

He's been reading every pregnancy and baby book that there is. It's always cute when he quotes them.

I yawn, and Kye moves back to my side.

"Did you want to hold her? Do you need anything?" He asks me, smoothing some of the hair away from my face.

"No, I'm good. Tired," I say, my eyes already closing.

"Get some sleep, darling. I've got this."

I smile, knowing that he does.

"Love you," I tell him sleepily.

"Love you more," he says, and I let those words echo in my head as I fall asleep.

Curious about Anson and Lottie's story? Check out A Baby For The Navy SEAL!

WANT A FREE BOOK?

You can grab Sweets Here.
Check out my website, www.shawhart.com for more free books!

ABOUT THE AUTHOR

CONNECT WITH ME!

If you enjoyed this story, please consider leaving a review on Amazon or any other reader site or blog that you like. Don't forget to recommend it to your other reader friends.

If you want to chat with me, please consider joining my VIP list or connecting with me on one of my Social Media platforms. I love talking with each of my readers. Links below!

<u>Website</u>
<u>Newsletter</u>

SERIES BY SHAW HART

Cherry Falls

803 Wishing Lane

1012 Curvy Way

Eye Candy Ink

Atlas

Mischa

Sam

Zeke

Nico

Eye Candy Ink: Second Generation

Ames

Harvey

Rooney

Gray

Ender

Banks

Fallen Peak

A Very Mountain Man Valentine's Day

A Very Mountain Man Halloween

A Very Mountain Man Thanksgiving

A Very Mountain Man Christmas

A Very Mountain Man New Year

Folklore

Kidnapping His Forever

Claiming His Forever

Finding His Forever

Rescuing His Forever

Chasing His Forever

Folklore: The Complete Series

Holiday Hearts

Be Mine

Falling in Love

Holly Jolly Holidays

Love Notes

Signing Off With Love

Care Package Love

Wrong Number, Right Love

Kings Gym

Fighting Fire With Fire

Fighting Tooth and Nail

Fighting Back From Hell

Mine To

Mine to Love

Mine to Protect

Mine to Cherish

Mine to Keep

Mine to: The Complete Series

Sequoia: Stud Farm

Branded

Bucked

Roped

Spurred

Sequoia: Fast Love Racing

Jump Start

Pit Stop

Home Stretch

Telltale Heart

Bought and Paid For

His Miracle

Pretty Girl

Telltale Hearts Boxset

ALSO BY SHAW HART

Still in the mood for Christmas books?

Stuffing Her Stocking, Mistletoe Kisses, Snowed in For Christmas, Coming Down Her Chimney.

Love holiday books? Check out these!

For Better or Worse, Riding His Broomstick, Thankful for His FAKE Girlfriend, His New Year Resolution, Hop Stuff, Taming Her Beast, Hungry For Dash, His Firework

Looking for some OTT love stories?

Her Scottish Savior, Baby Mama, Tempted By My Roommate, Blame It On The Rum, Wild Ride, Always

Looking for a celebrity love story?

Bedroom Eyes, Seducing Archer, Finding Their Rhythm

In the mood for some young love books?

Study Dates, His Forever, My Girl

Some other books by Shaw:

The Billionaire's Bet, Her Guardian Angel, Falling Again, Stealing Her, Dreamboat, Making Her His, Trouble

Printed in Great Britain
by Amazon